10657901

The Pedlar
of Swaffham

Other brilliant stories to collect:

The Pedlar
of Swaffham

Retold by
Philippa Pearce

Illustrated by
Rosamund Fowler

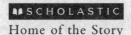

Home of the Story

Scholastic Children's Books,
Commonwealth House, 1–19 New Oxford Street,
London WC1A 1NU, UK
a division of Scholastic Ltd
London ~ New York ~ Toronto ~ Sydney ~ Auckland
Mexico City ~ New Delhi ~ Hong Kong

First published by Scholastic Ltd, 2001

Text copyright © Philippa Pearce, 2001
Illustrations copyright © Rosamund Fowler, 2001

ISBN 0 439 99923 5

All rights reserved

Printed by Cox and Wyman Ltd, Reading, Berks.

2 4 6 8 10 9 7 5 3 1

The right of Philippa Pearce and Rosamund Fowler to be identified as
the author and illustrator respectively of this work has been asserted by
them in accordance with the Copyright, Designs and Patents Act, 1988.

This book is sold subject to the condition that it shall not, by way
of trade or otherwise, be lent, resold, hired out, or otherwise
circulated without the publisher's prior consent in any form of
binding or cover other than that in which it is published and
without a similar condition, including this condition, being imposed
upon the subsequent purchaser.

Long ago, in the little town of Swaffham in Norfolk, a young man called Jack lived with his widowed mother. "Lived" is perhaps not quite the right word, for Jack was mostly away from home. He was a pedlar: he went on foot far and wide among

villages and remote homesteads to sell the goods that he carried in a pack on his back — ribbons and laces and gloves and caps and purses and belts and knives and needles and pins. He also sold little wooden things he had carved, such as whistles and pegs and tiny toys for children.

Jack was away for weeks on end. But when he returned, he always brought back to his mother some of the money from his trading. She still complained that he was so seldom at home. Their cottage needed its roof mending, she said; and their garden needed digging.

All that grew in it were a row of cabbages and a huge old oak tree.

One night when Jack was at home, he had a strange dream. He dreamed that he and his dog, Mal, were standing on a great bridge over a wide river — a bridge and a river that he had certainly never seen before. The strangest thing about the bridge was that it had houses and shops and even

a chapel built all along its span. "But, of course, this is only a dream," said Jack to himself, from inside his dream. Then he seemed to hear a voice – but was it really a voice, or just a *feeling*? – telling him that this was London Bridge. If he went there and waited on it for three days, he would hear something greatly to his advantage.

"What rubbish!" said Jack to himself, when he woke. But, for some reason, he remembered the dream. That day he dug and weeded his mother's garden and sowed some beans for her.

The next night, as soon as he fell asleep, he began dreaming exactly as before. He must go to London Bridge and wait there until he heard his great good news. This was the second night that he had dreamed the same dream.

The next day he began mending his mother's roof; but he worked slowly and did not finish the job. His mind was on other things. He could not get

the strangeness of the twice-dreaming out of his head. That night – the third night – he dreamed again of London Bridge and of the news that would come to him there.

This time, when he woke, he had made up his mind. "Nothing venture, nothing have!" he said to his dog, Mal. "We'll go to London, and – leaky roof or no leaky roof – we'll go now."

He said nothing to anyone of his great intention. He made up his pedlar's pack as usual and slung it on to his back. Then he took up his stout stick, called his dog to him, and said

goodbye to his lamenting mother, all just as usual.

Then together the pedlar and his dog set off to walk to London.

As he went, Jack stopped often, as usual, to sell goods from his pack — here a new cap for a young girl's betrothal, there a knife to replace one lost in the haymaking, and so on. At first he was selling to customers not

far from home who knew Jack well. After the bargaining was done, they talked of this and that, and Jack let slip that he was on his way to London. They were amazed and respectful. An old man who, in his youth, had driven flocks of geese from Norfolk to London said that the distance must be near a hundred miles, as the crow flies. Earnestly they all wished Jack good luck, and one of them gave his dog a bone before they left.

On such an expedition, Jack's dog, Mal, was the best of dogs. For mile after mile he trotted at his master's

side or at his heels. He was alert for everything that Jack did or said. If Jack stopped, he stopped. If Jack laid finger to lip, Mal sank to the ground, quiet as quiet, but ready – ready – "Go!" shouted Jack suddenly and Mal would spring like an arrow from the bow to chase the rabbit or hare or grey partridge that had started up in front of them. He usually caught what he hunted, and then later Jack would make a little fire of twigs and broken dead branches, and he and his dog would feast on roast meat that night. After supper, Jack

and his dog would sleep out in the open under the stars.

For the first few days the weather was fine, birds sang, and Jack whistled as he strode along. Then it began to rain; it drizzled; it poured. The roads, which were not much more than rutted tracks, anyway, became quagmires. Jack passed carts and wagons that had broken down, stuck deep in

the mud. Even riders on horseback had to pick their way carefully. But Jack, with two strong legs and his stick to help him trudged bravely on through slush and sludge and slime, with Mal padding along behind him.

Whether Jack spent the night in the open or under cover, Mal guarded him as he slept. If Jack left his pack even for a few minutes, he would say to Mal "On guard!" and Mal would stand over it, watchful. If any stranger approached, he bared his teeth in a snarl and growled deep in his throat. And what Mal threatened, he could do, too.

As they plodded on, they met other travellers, and Jack noticed that people were often surprised that he was bound for London from as far away as Swaffham in Norfolk. They wondered why. But he was careful to keep to himself the secret of his three dreams; and Mal, being a dog, never blabbed. All the same, Jack

decided in the end that it was perhaps better not even to mention Swaffham and Norfolk. Henceforth he kept to that resolve.

Now, at last, after many days of walking, in fair weather or foul, they were nearing London. People began to tell Jack to look out for the River Thames, on whose banks London stands. They gave him exact directions for finding London Bridge, built over the River. They told him that the Bridge was a wonderful sight, such as he could never even have dreamed of.

Jack smiled to himself, but all he

said was, "I mean to stand upon the Bridge."

"You do that," they said in such a kindly way that Jack knew they thought he must be simple-minded.

When Jack at last reached the Bridge, it was just as he had seen it in his dreams. There were buildings all along it, and, on the River below, boats of all kinds were passing up and

down under its arches. He walked to the middle of the Bridge and stopped. He stood there with Mal, staring round him, waiting for something to happen.

Nothing happened.

People passed him on the Bridge, hurrying to and fro, sparing him neither glance nor word. After a while, Jack realised how tired he was after so many days of walking, walking, walking. Now he did not need to walk anywhere, any more; here he was; here he must wait. He took off his pack – almost empty by now – and laid it down. "On guard!" he said to Mal.

Then he slid to the ground, until he could sit with his back resting against the front of a butcher's shop. There he sat, and allowed himself to fall asleep. Nobody paid any attention to him, except for the butcher, who peered out at him and thought what an idle fellow he must be.

At the end of that day, Jack had to get food and shelter for himself and his

dog. He could buy what little he needed – mostly bread and cheese; and he found shelter.

The next day Jack and Mal went early to the Bridge, to be sure of missing nothing. Jack stationed himself in the same place as before, by the butcher's shop. He wondered whether perhaps the butcher might spare Mal a bone; and when he caught his eye, he grinned at him. The butcher did not smile back. To tell the truth, he was beginning to be irritated that such an idle young man and his ill-tempered-looking cur should lounge about just

outside his shop.

And on this second day, again, nothing happened.

On the third day Jack and his dog were on the Bridge, as before. But today Jack did not feel like smiling at anybody or anything. Gloomily he had begun to think and to reason. If he were to receive this great good news, why could it not have come on the first

day of his waiting on the Bridge? Or at least on the second day? And here was the third and last day, and no sign whatsoever of message or messenger.

Meanwhile, the butcher's irritation had been rising ever higher at the sight of a pedlar and his dog planted on the very threshold of his premises. He could bear it no longer: he popped out of his shop to speak to Jack.

"I've been watching you," he said.

"Oh?" said Jack, and Mal growled softly.

"You may carry a pedlar's pack," said the butcher, "but you're selling nothing. You could be a beggar, but I've not caught you begging. What are you? A trickster? A thief? A slitter of throats in the night?"

"I'm an honest man," protested Jack. "I'm up from the country on an errand. I was told to come here."

"Did someone tell you that the streets of London are paved with gold?" sneered the butcher. "That's what all

you country bumpkins seem to believe."

"No, indeed," said Jack. "I was told only to come to London Bridge and wait here for news that would be to my advantage. But," he ended sadly, "no messenger has come."

"You were told – you were told – who told you this taradiddle?"

Jack hesitated. Then he said: "It was in a dream."

The butcher burst out laughing. "In a dream! You've come all this way because of a dream!" He stopped guffawing at last, wiped his eyes, and began to shake a finger at Jack. "Now I'll tell you something, young man. You're not the only one to have dreams. The other night I had a dream that I can still remember. I stood in the garden of some tumbledown cottage a long way from here in a place — why, I even remember the name: it was Soffam, or something like, in the county of Norfolk. An old woman lived in the cottage, and she had this

wretched garden with only a row of cabbages and a great old oak tree. Oh! and someone had sown a row of beans there, and one or two of them were just coming up. Now, don't interrupt, young man!"

For by this point in the butcher's account of his dream, Jack's mouth had fallen wide open, but it was with astonishment, not with any thought

of speaking. He was too dumbfounded for that.

"In my dream," continued the butcher, "I heard a voice – no, it was not really a voice at all – it was just a *feeling*, if you please! A *feeling* that if I dug under that oak tree in that garden I should find treasure! A treasure of gold!"

The butcher paused, aware that Jack was staring at him, speechless.

"Now," said the butcher, "you see standing before you a Londoner, not one of your clodhopping country cousins. Oh, no! I'm a Londoner, and

we Londoners know what's what. I'm not likely to be taken in by any foolish dream, am I? Answer me that! Am I?"

Jack started awake from his trance of amazement. "Oh, no – no – no – no – no! Certainly not!"

"So will this foolish dream send me gadding out of London into the back of beyond, to try to find a wretched little piece of nowhere with an oak tree growing in it? Now will it – will it?"

"I should hope not," said Jack. "With all my heart I should hope not!"

"So take my advice, young man," said the butcher, "and profit by my example. Wait here no longer for good news that never comes. Get you home as fast as you can, and be wiser than you have been."

Jack thanked the butcher humbly for his advice and promised to follow it. He and his dog would leave London at once and set off for home.

"And where's home, then?" asked the butcher, but Jack was suddenly very busy slinging his pack on to his back and finding his stick again. He called Mal to him, although Mal was always ready, anyway. Hurriedly Jack said: "Oh, it's near a hundred miles from here, as the crow flies. Come, Mal – we're off, we're off!"

"But you didn't say where you're from exactly," said the butcher.

"I didn't say," answered Jack, "because I'm so seldom there. Truly, I'm a pedlar. I wander here, there and everywhere selling from my pack.

I sell ribbons – laces – gloves – caps –
purses – belts – knives – needles – pins.
Oh, and I sell–"

"Yes, yes!" the butcher interrupted.
"I don't need to know all that!" He
forgot his question about Jack's home,
in the bustle that Jack was making
about his departure. Now, in great
haste, Jack was bidding goodbye to
the butcher, thanking him yet again.

The butcher watched them go, pleased that a young man should be so grateful for advice – which not everybody was, in his experience. He had even thought for a moment of going back into his shop to get a bone for the young man's dog, but thought better of it. The young man's folly should not seem to be rewarded in any way. Besides, one could sell bones. And already the pedlar was out of earshot, hurrying off the Bridge with his dog, on his way home – wherever that was.

For Jack, his only thought was to

get home as fast as he could, to the oak tree in his mother's garden. He was in a fever to get there. As they left the Bridge behind them for the streets of London, he saw a bird mounting into the sky ahead of them – a crow, and he seemed to hear his own voice saying to the butcher, "near a hundred miles from here, as the crow flies."

If only he could fly!

He put all such nonsense from his mind, and settled to a steady pace for the many miles ahead. During the day, he and his dog rested seldom; in the mornings, they set off before daybreak, and at the end of every day they walked well on into dusk and even nightfall.

Day after day they pressed on, through fair weather and foul, until at last, with the sun setting behind them, they came to familiar sights.

"Look ahead, Mal! There's a ruined tower that you and I know well!" And there before them was Swaffham

church tower, and this was Swaffham, and here was the old widow woman's cottage, and Jack and Mal broke into a run and burst in through the door just as Jack's mother was taking a steaming pot of soup from the fire.

The old woman was almost startled out of her wits — but never spilled the soup — when Jack appeared so suddenly before her. He was travel-stained, and

gaunt and grey with exhaustion and hunger; and Mal was in no better state. Jack's eyes glittered in a strange excitement, and he babbled of London Bridge and a butcher – and then abruptly would say nothing more at all.

For suddenly the thought had come into Jack's head that the dreams might, after all, be what the butcher had called them: mere foolishness – a cruel joke.

So he did not speak to his mother of buried treasure, nor rush out to the huge old oak tree. He sat on his usual stool, and drank his soup, and fed

Mal, and listened to his mother talking of her leaky roof and of her beans that were coming up in the garden.

When his mother went to bed, he stayed sitting on his stool by the fire. There he sat, in spite of his tiredness, until he was sure his mother was asleep – until he heard her snoring.

Then he crept out of the cottage, picking up a spade from among his

mother's tools as he went. Mal followed him.

The moon shone.

Jack began to dig under the oak tree. He dug here and he dug there, and sometimes his spade struck a stone and often his spade struck a tree-root. He dug deeper here and deeper there, and his spade struck more stones and more tree-roots.

Then suddenly — "Aha!" Jack said so softly that only Mal could hear him. For Jack's spade had struck something that was neither stone nor root. It seemed as if it might be metal. Jack

dug around whatever it was, until he could get his arm down the hole and feel with his hand.

"There is something!" he told Mal, and Mal crept closer and whined. "It's a curved metal rim of something… why, the curve goes all round – it's the rim of some kind of pot. And the pot's full of something!"

First of all there was earth and earthy rubbish, and then – tightly packed – came small round flat things. Jack brought up one of these things and held it up in the moonlight. It was encrusted and black, but Jack

scratched at it with his fingernail and
rubbed it against his jacket. Lo and
behold! there was a gleam of something unmistakable –

"Gold!" whispered Jack.

Then Jack dug and dug, until at last
he could heave out of the earth a great
brass pot – far bigger than his
mother's stew-pot – full to the brim
with gold coins. It had been hidden

there long ago, who could tell by whom?

So the double dreamings had come true; and Jack became a rich man. In thanksgiving he rebuilt the tower of Swaffham church, and also its north aisle. He did not finish mending his mother's cottage roof, because he built her a whole new cottage, bigger and better, but with the same garden. He married a wife and they lived in a good house, and had many children. He did not forget his dog, Mal. Mal had a bone every day of his life, and when he died, he was buried under the huge oak tree.